Shola's Game

a novel

by

SHAWN DURKIN

H•I•P Books

HIP Sr.

Library and Archives Canada Cataloguing in Publication

Durkin, Shawn, 1971–
    Shola's game / Shawn Durkin.

(New Series Canada)
ISBN 1-897039-17-4

    I. Title. II. Series.

PS8607.U756S56 2006   jC813'.6   C2006-900841-8

General editor: Paul Kropp
Text design: Laura Brady
Illustrations drawn by: Catherine Doherty
Cover design: Robert Corrigan

1 2 3 4 5 6 7   07 06 05 04 03 02

Printed and bound in Canada

High Interest Publishing acknowledges the financial support of the
Government of Canada through the Book Publishing Industry
Development Program (BPIDP) for our publishing activities.

Shola has just come to Canada. He feels like an outsider. Back in Nigeria, he was a soccer star, but now he has to learn a new sport. Will hockey help him feel at home here?

CHAPTER 1

The First Goal

Shola blocked the shot with his shin pads. He took off after the puck, catching up to it at centre ice. He had a breakaway. A few more strides and he was closing in on goal.

The goalie looked very much alone, way out in front of his net.

If only my old friends could see me now, Shola said to himself. He was skating on a sheet of ice. He was playing a game none of his friends had ever

heard of. He was playing this game in a cold, cold country, so far from where he was born.

And now, he might just score the winning goal.

Shola glanced up at the clock. Twenty seconds. Plenty of time. He thought for a second, then launched his attack. Shola cut to his right and then to his left. This brought him across the face of the goal and forced the goalkeeper to move with him. This had been his favourite move in soccer, back in his old country. Why wouldn't it work in hockey?

Shola cut in front. The puck seemed to slide off his stick and back into his skates.

The goalie froze. His eyes lit up as he saw Shola's "mistake." He got ready to launch himself at the puck, to clear it out of the way. But just as the goalie threw himself forward, Shola used his back skate to kick the puck up to his stick.

There was the net, wide and empty.

Shola smiled. The goalie gritted his teeth.

Six months ago, Shola had arrived for his first day at Burrard High. He was terrified. A new school is bad enough. But this new school was in a new country.

Shola and his family had just come to Canada. This new land seemed very strange. All these new things: DVDs, cars, fast food, iPods! Shola's family talked each night about the new life they were living. So far they had faced it together, and they had all been fine. But school was something that Shola had to face by himself.

Back in Nigeria, Shola's school had been a

group of outdoor classrooms in a big green field. The classrooms had roofs to protect students from the sun and rain, but no walls. The teacher stood at a blackboard on wheels to write lessons. The students sat in rows facing her, two to a desk. All the children wore the school uniform – a light blue T-shirt and dark blue shorts. Only the teachers wore shoes. Only the teachers *had* shoes.

Burrard High was half a world away from the village where Shola had grown up. This school was a big building with brick walls, long hallways and noisy stairwells. It made Shola feel small and scared.

Shola had come to school in a pair of jeans and a long-sleeved shirt. It felt strange, but this is what kids wore here. Strangest of all were the shoes on his feet. In this new country, all the kids wore shoes. Shola kept rubbing his feet together, as if to make sure the shoes were still there.

Shola walked through the halls with a lady from the office. The other kids kept staring at them. Did he look that strange? At last he made it to the first-period classroom. The teacher was a tall, smiling woman wearing a blue dress. She stood beside a desk. The class was set out in rows with one student at each desk.

"This is a new student," she told the class. "His name is Shola."

All the other kids were looking at him and some were grinning. Were these friendly smiles? Or were they making fun of him?

"Nice name," someone whispered.

The teacher glared at the class. Then she pointed toward an empty desk halfway down the far row. Shola walked down the row, avoiding the eyes staring at him. At last, the teacher started a math lesson. Shola, glad to have something to do, opened his book.

"Shola," he heard again. The voice was still a whisper. "What kind of stupid name is that?"

Shola kept his eyes on his book, but his heart was aching. Why had he come so far for this?

CHAPTER 2

Like a Nail Through His Foot

At lunch, Shola followed the other kids outside. Behind the school was a sight that Shola knew well – a soccer field. A game was going on. Kids were running up and down, chasing the ball and calling out to each other. Shola went over to watch.

He stood off to one side, feeling awkward. His shoes hurt. His eyes scanned the field, but he was too shy to join in. The other guys would stare at him. *Shola*, he remembered, *what kind of stupid name is that?*

Shola waited. Time dragged. At last Shola heard his name called out.

"Shola, you want to play?" It was a guy with straight red hair and freckles. Shola had seen him in his math class.

Shola looked up and down the field, then back at the boy. Was he making fun of him? No, Shola decided.

"Come on, you're on our team. We're going that way." The redhead pointed down to the far end.

"Yes, yes," Shola said. Then he felt foolish for repeating himself.

Shola ran out and started running down the field. This game he knew. This game made sense – not like his new school and new country. This was a game Shola had played all his life.

But there was a problem. Shola's new shoes seemed heavy on his feet. He felt clumsy trying to run in them. He couldn't set up a play. He couldn't even catch up with the ball.

What would I do at home? Shola asked himself.

The answer was simple. He ran over to the sidelines and kicked off his shoes. He peeled off his socks, too, and ran back out onto the field.

Shola felt much better without shoes on. Soon he was in the middle of the action. He blocked the ball down near his own goal and kicked it way up the field. The next time he got the ball, Shola controlled it like a pro.

"Way to go," shouted one of the guys.

Shola moved to his right and found himself in empty space. Looking up, he saw the red-haired kid who had asked him to play. Shola quickly passed him the ball. It was a good kick that landed right at the redhead's feet. The guy turned and started running toward the goal. He passed to a girl on the side who steadied herself and kicked the ball into the corner of the net.

A cheer went up from Shola's team.

Shola noticed the red-haired boy running back toward him. "Hey, Shola," he said, "nice pass." Still running, the boy held up his hand as if to wave.

Shola held up his hand too, in response. The red-haired boy ran past him and slapped Shola's open

11

hand with his own. Shola looked down at his hand, surprised. It seemed such a strange thing to do.

The other team kicked the ball down the field and Shola went running after it. He got control and tried to run with the ball. But before he could take a step, he felt a heavy boot stomp down on his foot.

It felt like someone had hammered nails through his foot. Shola was too stunned to shout, too surprised to cry. He limped forward, then fell to the ground in pain.

Shola looked up to see a big kid with brown hair looking down at him. The guy was laughing. "Better get yourself some shoes, or you might get hurt," the kid said.

Shola jumped up to show him that he was okay, but the guy had run off.

Shola wanted to yell something at him. He wanted to swear like these Canadian kids, but he didn't know the words. So he just stood there, his face burning.

Shola got back in the game and played well. He kept away from the kid who had stepped on his foot.

When the game was over, the redhead came up

beside him. "Amazing," he said as they did the strange hand-slap again. "My name's Turner by the way," said the red-haired boy. "I'm in your math class."

"I thought you must be," said Shola. "Nobody else knows my name."

Turner laughed. "They will pretty soon – if you keep playing soccer like that." He pointed down at Shola's feet. "How can you play barefoot? Doesn't it hurt?"

They stopped briefly to pick up Shola's shoes and socks. "Not really," Shola replied, "I guess you just have to get used to it."

Shola looked down at Turner's feet. He was wearing white running shoes with rubber soles and swoops of colour down the sides. They looked light and fast, just the thing for running.

Then Shola looked at his own shoes. They were brown and heavy and clunky, with thin black laces. His mother was so proud when she bought them. "You must have good, sturdy shoes," she told him.

But today Shola hated them. *Will I ever fit in here?* Shola wondered.

The next day, it rained. There was no soccer game out in the field. Instead, Shola sat next to Turner in the school lunchroom. He put his brown paper bag on the table and pulled out a blue plastic box.

"Cool shirt, by the way," said Turner, unpacking his own lunch. "You didn't say you were into Power Command."

Shola looked down at his shirt. The picture was of a gleaming white spaceship set against a backdrop of stars. Shola had picked the shirt himself but had no idea what it meant. He looked at Turner. "Power Command?" he asked.

"Yeah, that's their ship, the Space Eagle. Don't tell me you've never played the game?"

Shola shook his head. He just liked the picture on the shirt. He'd never even *heard* of the game.

Turner looked surprised. "Well, I've got it at home. You're going to have to come over and play it."

Just then they heard a voice from behind, asking them to make some room. They both turned around. "Oh, hi, Janna," said Turner. They moved over to let her sit down.

Shola remembered this girl. She was the one who had scored the goal in their soccer game.

"Hi, Shola," said the girl. "How's it going so far? Still feeling kind of weird?"

Shola nodded. "Well, it's very . . . um, well . . . ."

Janna giggled. "Don't worry, I know how you feel. I came here just two years ago, but it seems like ages," she said. "Nice shirt, by the way. Power Command is, like, way cool."

"He doesn't know what it is," mumbled Turner. His mouth was full of sandwich.

Janna looked shocked. "Doesn't know?" she said. "It's, like, only the best game ever. Didn't they have X-Box games in your country?"

Shola shook his head. In Nigeria, they felt lucky when there was power for the lights. His family had a TV and that made them rich. Here, people had TVs in their cars and telephones in their pockets.

Shola opened the lid of his blue lunch box. He knew what would be inside – the one dish his mother had learned to make since coming here. Shola began to eat with a plastic fork.

After a few seconds, he could feel that Janna

and Turner were staring. They both looked at him, then back at the food in his blue lunch box. Macaroni and cheese. Cold.

Turner shook his head, then reached into his own lunch box. He pulled out half a sandwich and offered it to Shola.

"Shola, there is one thing you've got to learn," he said. "Cold macaroni and cheese . . . it's the grossest thing ever."

CHAPTER 3

Hockey? What's Hockey?

By November, it was starting to get cold. Shola had never felt cold like this. It was like being inside a fridge all the time, only outside. In the mornings he would go off to school in many layers of clothes. Still, he could feel himself freezing where his skin touched the air.

One day, Turner joined Shola for the morning walk wearing a new jacket. The jacket was blue with red stripes on the shoulders and a crest on the front left. On the back was written "Rangers" in big letters. Shola asked Turner where he could buy a jacket like that.

"One of these?" Turner said, holding out his arms. "You don't just go out and buy one of these. You've got to earn it."

Shola was surprised. "Earn it? How would I do that?"

Turner smiled. "You've got to play for a team, that's how. This is the hockey team I play for, the Rangers."

"Hockey team? More like the jerk team," came a voice from behind them. "Or maybe this barefoot boy is going to play for you. Maybe he can skate in his bare feet."

Turner and Shola looked around. Standing next to them was the guy who had stepped on Shola's foot. He was with a group of tough-looking kids. All those guys were wearing jackets like Turner's, but in green. The letters on the back spelled out "Chargers."

Turner's mouth twisted. Shola could tell he was angry. "I guess we'll find out on Saturday, eh?"

"You know we will," said the guy. The group forced Turner and Shola to step off the path. They had a strange walk, Shola thought, like the walk of singers on music videos.

"That's Keith," said Turner once the gang had passed. "He tries to be a bully, but mostly he's harmless. We're playing his team on Saturday. It's the first game of the hockey season."

Shola nodded his head. "Turner, I have a small question – what's hockey?"

Turner looked at him, amazed. "What's hockey?" Turner asked, his voice rising. "*What's hockey?*" he repeated. "You've been in this country for four months and you still don't know? I mean, that's like asking, what's breathing? Hockey is just about the greatest sport there is!"

Shola gave a little laugh. "Better than soccer? I don't think so."

Turner grinned. "Better, faster and way cooler."

"Not possible," Shola replied.

"I tell you what," said Turner. "Come by my place after school and I'll show you the basics."

When he arrived at Turner's house, Shola was

surprised to see Turner turn off the Power Command game. Turner opened a drawer and flipped through some other disks. At last he found the one he was looking for and put it in the X-Box. *Big League Hockey* came up on the screen.

Turner handed Shola a controller. "We'll start out at the lowest level until you pick up the rules."

Shola figured out the rules soon enough. At a basic level, hockey was much like soccer. The object was for a team to score in the other team's goal, shooting it past their goaltender and into a net. Shola was surprised at how the players banged and crashed into each other, but he got used to it. Soon, his players were giving as good as they got.

"That's the end of lesson one," said Turner as they packed up the game. "Lesson two is on Saturday night. Come and watch the real thing."

"Your game against Keith's team?"

Turner nodded. "My dad will give you a lift to the arena. Pick you up at 6:30."

So on Saturday, Shola sat up in the stands with Turner's dad. It was cold in the arena. Shola had to blow on his fingers to keep warm.

Then the Rangers and the Chargers skated out on the ice. The Rangers wore blue shirts trimmed with red. The players all looked the same in their uniforms and helmets, but Shola knew that his friend was wearing number 11. The Chargers were wearing green and yellow. Shola could tell by his size that Keith was wearing number 5.

Once the game started, Shola could hardly believe his eyes. The players moved like a whirlwind as they chased the puck back and forth. Everything happened so fast it was hard for Shola to keep up. He was amazed at the skill the players used to control the puck. He wondered how they could bounce right back to their feet after being knocked over. Before he knew it, a loud buzzer went off. It was the end of the first period and the score was still tied at zero.

The second period was just as fast as the first. Shola noticed that Keith was using his size and playing rough, knocking into people every chance he got. It seemed to pay off, though. Keith scored the first goal of the game after knocking a Rangers' player off the puck.

Later on, Turner pounced on a loose puck and skated up the ice with it. He drove down the boards toward the corner, with a defenceman coming up fast. Turner flicked the puck toward the front of the net, just in time for a teammate to pick it up. It was that guy who fired the puck past the goalie and into the net.

Shola jumped up and cheered with the rest of the Rangers' fans. The game was now tied 1–1.

Late in the third period, Turner once again started a rush out of his own end. He made a great pass to his winger, who kept bringing the puck forward. Then Keith moved across and skated right into the winger. This knocked the guy down and sent the puck flying free. Turner picked it up on his way past, then drove to the net. He passed and received a great pass back, right on his stick. In a flash, Turner went around the goalie and put it in the net. 2–1 Rangers.

Before Turner could even see the new score, he was hit from behind. Keith came at him full force and knocked him into the boards.

The crowd's cheers turned into silence as

Turner fell to the ice.

The coach and other players ran over. Shola was ready to go jumping out of the stands to help. But before Shola could move, Turner got up, holding his shoulder. The coach helped Turner back to the bench. From the way Turner moved, it was clear that he was really in pain.

Of course, the referee sent Keith off the ice. This forced the Chargers to play one man short for the rest of the game, so it was no surprise when the Rangers won. But Shola no longer cared about the game. He rushed down after the final buzzer to see his friend.

Turner came out of the dressing room holding his left forearm in his right hand. "It might be a broken collarbone," said Turner's dad. "We've got to get an x-ray but we'll drop you at home first."

Shola nodded, then looked at Turner. His friend was in real pain but still smiling.

"So what do you think Shola?" Turner asked. "Better than soccer?"

"This would never happen in soccer," Shola replied.

"But answer my question. What did you think?"

Shola seemed at a loss for words. "It was . . . wild. So fast, and . . . well, cool, until that guy hit you."

"Want to learn the real game?" Turner asked.

Shola just stood there, his mouth open.

Turner laughed. "Looks like I'm going to have a few weeks off the ice," he said. "I've got time to teach you a thing or two."

CHAPTER 4

A Natural

The first step in learning how to play, Turner told Shola, was learning how to skate. But first Shola needed a pair of skates. His feet were much larger than Turner's, so he couldn't borrow his skates. Instead, Shola had to talk to his dad.

"Shola, I'm not sure about you playing this game," his father said. "Your friend Turner has been hurt. I've seen those hockey players fight on TV. Why can't you wait for the summer and play soccer?"

"But Dad," moaned Shola. He used this short form now, not *father*, like he used to. "This game is just like soccer but so much faster. It's so much more fun."

Shola's father was still not sure, but he saw the spark in his son's eyes. He wanted Shola to be happy in their new country. Maybe this strange ice game was how the kids had fun here.

So the next day, Shola and his father went out to buy a pair of skates. They took the bus to a mall at the south side of town.

"Canadian Tire," muttered Shola's dad. "A tire store for ice skates?"

"Turner says there's a sale," Shola replied.

The two of them walked to the sports section. "More skates here than tires," said Shola's dad. He seemed surprised. "How about a nice white pair, like these?"

"Those are figure skates," Shola told him.

"They seem very nice."

Shola sighed. "They're for girls, Dad."

Shola picked a pair of Bauer skates that were on sale. Still, his father was shocked at the price. "This

is an expensive game," said his dad. "Don't tell your mother what they cost."

Shola said nothing. He loved the feel of his new skates and held them tightly all the way home. The boots were stiff and hard but they had felt pretty good on his feet. The blades underneath were cold to the touch, smooth and sharp on the edges. Shola could picture himself sliding over the ice.

Close to Turner's house there was a park with an outdoor rink. When Shola and Tuner arrived, there were just a few people skating around. Shola was glad that so few people would see his first try at skating.

Shola had to help Turner tie his laces because his friend's arm was still in a sling. Then he tied the laces on his own skates, and Turner bent down to tighten them. Standing by the side of the rink Shola felt scared. Shola was already tall, but the skates made him taller. He was having trouble balancing on just two thin blades.

"Don't worry," said Turner. "It's easier than it looks." With a step, Turner was on the ice, gliding in a small circle back to where Shola stood.

Shola watched the easy move. How could he ever do that?

Just then, a kid in a green jacket came around the corner. It was Keith, the bully, with several of his friends. Shola froze.

"What do we have here?" called Keith. "Looks like a cripple trying to teach a barefoot boy how to skate."

Shola felt the blood rushing to his face.

"Ignore them," Turner whispered.

"Hey, cripple," called out Keith. "How's your shoulder?" Keith and his friends laughed again.

"It'll be fine next time we play you," Turner called back. "Don't you worry."

"Oh, I'm not worried," called Keith. "I'm just hoping to finish the job."

Turner turned back to Shola, his face red with anger. He was trying to follow his own advice – ignore them.

"So let's see your girlfriend skate!" Keith called. He and his friends had lined up on their side of the ice. They were watching Shola closely.

Turner shrugged. "Show them you can skate,"

Turner said simply. Then he stepped out of Shola's way.

Shola took a deep breath. This was it. He stepped forward, pushing off with his back foot. The blade dug into the ice, then glided. He was skating! He was doing it! In front of Keith and his friends too.

Then Shola put his left foot down. Suddenly his legs were going in two different directions at once. In an instant, his feet kicked up in the air. He was flying . . . and turning . . . until he fell hard on his butt.

Keith and his friends burst out laughing. They were doubling over and slapping each other on the back.

Turner came skating over. Shola was upset to see that even his friend was smiling.

"Come on," laughed Turner, "it did look pretty funny. Besides, it only gets better from here." He offered his good hand and helped Shola to his feet.

Turner started teaching Shola how to skate. He showed him how to keep his balance and how to transfer his weight. Keith and his friends soon lost interest and wandered off. But Shola didn't see that.

He was watching Turner and learning fast. By the end of their first session, Shola was able to go all the way around the rink without falling.

"You're doing great," Turner told him as they took off their skates. "Now all you need is practice. Lots of practice."

Every morning after that, Shola woke up early and made his way to the park. Sometimes Turner would join him, but mostly Shola was on his own. He would skate up and down, getting faster and faster on the ice. He worked hard on stops and turns as his balance got better. When he went back home for breakfast, his teeth were often chattering and his toes and fingers were numb.

"Are you sure you want to do this?" his father would ask. "We can still return the skates."

But his mother would fuss over him. She'd wrap him in a blanket and give him cups of hot tea until he had to go to school. "Just don't get hurt on the ice," she'd say.

"I won't get hurt," he said. "I promise."

Turner kept giving Shola lessons after school. The redhead couldn't believe how fast his friend was learning. It wasn't very long before Shola was skating like he had been doing it for years.

"You skate like Mats Sundin," Turner said.

"Who's Mats Sundin?" Shola asked, and Turner just sighed.

One day, when Shola headed to the park for a skating lesson, Turner called him back. "No skating today, Shola," he said. "Time to move on to the next level."

They made their way to Turner's house where they opened the garage. Against the back wall, painted on the bricks, was the outline of a hockey net. It even had a life-sized painted goalie. "Wow," exclaimed Shola, looking at the crouching goalie, "that's wild!"

"Yeah. Dad made it for me when I was little. It helped me a lot with my shooting. I figure it will help you, too."

Shola was a bit confused. "It helped with your shooting? How?"

Turner grabbed a hockey stick and several

pucks from the corner of the garage. In a flash, he brought the stick back and slapped at a puck. The puck whizzed past Shola and hit the back wall between the parted pads of the painted goalie.

Turner grinned at Shola. "Target practice!" he said.

Looking back at the painted wall, Shola could see that some parts of the net weren't covered by the goalie. Between the goalie's pads and in each of the four corners, there were black rubber marks where countless pucks had hit the brick. *So that's how they score a goal,* Shola thought.

He looked up at Turner. "Let me try," he said.

Turner handed him a stick and showed him how to hold it. Then he put a puck on the floor and stood back.

"Now you probably won't be able to shoot very hard at first," he said. "So just try and get the feel for the puck on the stick. Try to relax and hit smooth."

Shola nodded. He looked at the puck, brought the stick back and swung hard. The puck flew off Shola's stick and hit the goalie right between the eyes.

"Wow!" said Turner, wide-eyed. "You trying to kill the guy? Try it again."

He set up another puck and Shola slapped it just as hard. He focused on keeping the puck low this time. The puck smacked between the goalie's pads, exactly where Turner's shot had hit.

Turner was amazed. "You're a natural, Shola! I've never seen anyone shoot so hard so fast."

Then, of course, Shola missed three shots in a row. But slowly he got better – better aim, better speed. He soon found the corners and the space between the pads. He really was a natural.

Shola and Turner stayed in the garage for hours. By the end of their first session, Shola was scoring nearly as many goals as Turner was. Later, Turner told Shola about the pick-up street hockey game at the school. "We'll go play this weekend. Just street hockey, but you'll learn a lot."

"A game?" Shola asked. "Do you think I'm ready?"

"You're a natural," Turner said. "Why wait?"

A natural? How could a kid from Nigeria be a natural at hockey? Skating and shooting was one thing, but playing in a game?

CHAPTER 5

Just a Down Payment

Shola and Turner walked up the path toward the school, their sticks over their shoulders. The pick-up game had already started. There were many more kids than Shola had seen in Turner's game at the rink. And these kids were using a tennis ball instead of a puck.

The boys waited on the sidelines for a break in play. Finally a big guy with long brown hair took a shot that just missed the net. The tennis ball went bouncing down the path where Shola and Turner had just walked.

The big guy swore as two younger kids tore off after the ball. Then the big guy raised his head and saw Shola and Turner waiting to get in the game. "Hey, Alex," he called to another guy. "How about you get these two and we get my brother when he gets here?"

Alex was a tall Asian kid with a lanky build. "Works for me. Hey, Turner, who's your friend?"

"Shola," Turner shouted back to him. "He's just learning."

"No problem," shouted Alex. "My sister's been playing for a year, and you couldn't be worse than her."

"Hey, shut up," came a shout from one side.

Shola looked over. It was Janna, the girl from school. Shola took a deep breath. He held his stick out in front of him as Turner had taught him. At least he didn't have to skate. This was only a tennis ball on pavement, just like soccer . . . almost.

Alex got the ball, turned, and began to run with it toward the goal. The ball seemed to float on the

end of his stick as he danced it back and forth. He passed the ball off, got it ball back and then sent it past the helpless goalie.

"Six to three?" said Alex. He was grinning at the big guy, a kid named Darcy.

"Yeah, yeah," grumbled Darcy. "Hey, there's my pukeface of a little brother. Hurry up, Keith! We're going to toast these guys."

Shola looked up. There was Keith, the bully, running into the game. Shola could almost feel the pain come back to his foot.

Shola hadn't been playing very hard. He'd been hanging around the edge of the game, mostly just watching. But now that Keith was in the game, Shola felt a need to do something. He ran in a few times and once bounced off Keith's shoulder and fell down. Keith was built like a rock.

Keith looked down at him and sneered. "Hey, who let the barefoot kid play?" he called out.

Shola was not barefoot, but still the comment hurt him.

"Shut up and play the game, Keith," ordered his brother.

A bit later, Shola was open when Alex turned and passed him the ball. Looking up, he saw every face in the game turn toward him. Shola was in front of the net and had an open shot.

By the time he made up his mind, it was too late. Keith came running toward him, stealing the ball off his stick. Then Keith ran down to the other end to score a breakaway goal.

Shola felt stupid. He had cost his team a goal.

"Thanks for the pass!" laughed Keith, running back past Shola.

Shola looked to Turner, but Turner just shrugged. "At least you can only get better!" Turner laughed.

Shola was even more determined to make up for his mistake. He chased the ball up and down, through a forest of legs and sticks. After a while, he got another pass when he was in scoring position.

Just as Shola swung, Keith ran in front of the net.

The ball moved very fast toward the top corner of the net. It seemed to be sailing right into the net, but then Keith jumped up and over to the left.

Whap! The ball hit Keith's butt with a loud slap.

Keith swore. He dropped his stick and grabbed the rear of his pants with his gloved hands. Then he whipped around and fixed his eyes on Shola.

"You're going to pay for that," Keith shouted. "You're going to be meat, just like your stupid friend."

Keith's older brother just laughed. "Cool it, puke face," Darcy told Keith. "Besides, it wasn't a bad save. I knew that big butt of yours had to be good for something."

Keith threw down his stick, but everyone else began to laugh. In a second, the game began again.

Both sides played hard. Keith took every chance to rush into Shola or send the ball sailing by Shola's head. It took another hour for Keith to get even. Shola was in front of his goal and Keith was coming at him, hard and fast. Shola moved to block, but Keith ducked his shoulder and came at him. Shola took the check in his chest. Then he lost his balance and fell back, sprawling on the pavement.

"That's just a down payment, guy," Keith swore. "If I ever play you on *real* ice, you're going to get hurt a lot more than that."

CHAPTER 6

You're Ready

Shola finally got a chance to play on real ice. He and Turner began to practise at the rink over Christmas vacation. For Turner, it was a chance to get his shoulder back in shape. For Shola, it was a chance to learn the real game.

Shola made good progress on the ice. He wasn't a great skater, but his shots were dead on and his passing was great. He seemed to have a real feel for the game.

In January, Turner went to his first practice since his injury. Shola saw him at school, right after the practice. "How'd it go?" Shola asked.

"No problems," Turner told him. "I'm back to my superstar best."

"That's good news," said Shola, pleased for his friend.

"Actually, the good news is for you," Turner told him. "I had a talk with our coach. I told him about this awesome new player I know. I told him the guy would be great on our team. So now he wants me to bring him to the next practice."

"So who's the new guy?" Shola asked.

Turner couldn't stop himself from laughing, "Why, it's you, of course!"

Shola was stunned. A tryout? With the Rangers? Surely Turner wasn't telling him the truth. "I . . . I don't know what to say. Thank you, but wow, the Rangers? I'm not ready."

"Hey," said Turner, "I'm your personal coach. If I say you're ready, you're ready."

Shola wasn't quite as certain. "Well, I guess, but. . . ."

"No buts. Just make the team and I'll be happy."

Shola nodded, and the bell for first class rang. Shola was feeling great all day. When he got home, he was excited to tell his parents about the tryout.

What surprised him was their response. Shola's mother shook her head and stamped her foot. "Absolutely not. No way!" she said. "It's one thing to skate with your friend, but a hockey team? I forbid it!"

Shola looked at his father, hoping for some support. His father had always been on his side, but now his father would not meet his eyes.

"Shola, your mother and I are worried about you getting hurt," said his father. "These other boys have been playing for a long time. Hockey is a very rough game. Just look how they play it on TV."

"But I can't just give it up," Shola moaned. "How can I get good at it if I don't try? I just want a chance."

Shola's parents looked at each other. They were worried about him. They knew how hard it had been for Shola to fit in. But he'd already been hurt in his pick-up games. They feared he'd be hurt again.

"No, Shola," said his mother. "You can skate with your friend, but no hockey games for a team. The answer is no."

His father folded his arms and looked away. The answer was clear.

Shola had never gone against his parents. He wasn't like some boys who lied to their mothers or did not listen to their fathers. He was a good son. He had made no trouble since coming to this new country. But now – this!

Shola made up his mind. He was going to try out for the Rangers. His parents didn't have to know. And his parents couldn't stop him from trying.

The days passed quickly and soon it was time for the Rangers' practice. Shola was nervous. He paced up and down in his living room, waiting for Turner and his dad to pick him up. When they finally arrived, Shola said a quick goodbye to his parents and dashed out the door. He told them he was going to watch Turner play. That much, at least, was the truth.

At the rink, Shola and Turner walked in

together, dragging their hockey gear. Shola stayed close to Turner.

"There he is," said Turner. "Come on."

They walked over to an older man in a Rangers jacket.

"Hey, Greg." called Turner. The man in the jacket looked up and offered a smile. "Turner," he said, "who's your friend?"

"This is the guy I was telling you about," Turner replied. "Shola, meet Greg – our coach."

Greg stuck out his hand. "I hear you want to play for the Rangers."

Shola shook his hand. "Yes, sir, I mean, if I can."

The coach laughed "Sir? What is this 'sir' stuff? Greg is fine. Or 'coach' if you want."

Shola smiled. "Okay, coach."

"That's better. Now let's see what you've got."

Turner had brought a set of hockey gear for Shola. "It's some of my old stuff and some of my brother's. Don't worry, it's all clean," he said.

The gear wasn't that clean, but it was good enough. After all, Shola wouldn't have gotten this far without Turner.

Shola was scared as he stepped out on the ice. He felt as if he couldn't skate at all, as if he'd never held a hockey stick before.

Turner could see the fear, even behind Shola's visor. "Hey, man," he said "I wouldn't have brought you here if I didn't think you could do it. Let's just have some fun, okay?"

Shola got over his panic. He watched the other players and tried to do what they did. He was glad that he could keep up with the speed of the skating drills. All those cold mornings in the park had paid off. Then the pucks came out and some passing drills began. That was harder. All the other players seemed to pass the pucks around easily. Shola had to focus hard and he let several passes go astray.

Finally the coach started a practice game. He put Shola on the wing with Turner as centre.

Turner skated over before they got started. "Hey, you're doing good."

"Do you think so?" Shola replied. "I'm not too sure."

"No sweat, my friend," Turner told him. "Just stay on your wing, chase the puck when it's on your side and cover that guy when we're on D. Think you can remember that?"

Shola nodded. "I hope so."

Turner tapped him with his stick. "Good. Now let's play some hockey."

Greg dropped the puck at centre and the game was underway. Turner won the face-off and passed back to Shola. Before Shola could turn or look up, he was knocked off his feet. The puck was gone in an instant.

Shola bounced up and went chasing after it. Although he skated as hard as he could, Shola couldn't control the puck. He was thinking too much. The game was too fast and it was taking too long for him to decide what to do.

Finally Greg blew the whistle to end the game. Shola was near centre ice and the puck drifted over to him. In pure frustration he swung his stick and hit the puck as hard as he could. It flew through the air and into the top corner of the net.

"Wow," said Greg as he came back to the group. "Great shot!"

After a few more skating drills, the practice was

over. Greg called Shola over while the other players left the ice. Shola skated over slowly, his head down. He knew he hadn't played well.

Greg looked stern. "Turner tells me you've only been skating for a month or two. Is that true?"

Shola looked up. "Yes. I practise every morning before school."

"Do you really?" Greg looked surprised. "So you've never played hockey before then?"

"Where I come from," Shola shrugged, "there is no hockey. We only play soccer."

"So where did you learn to shoot like that?"

"In Turner's garage."

Greg looked thoughtful. "I've got to be honest Shola. You might be a very good player some day. But right now, you don't have the speed or the eye for the puck. A great shot is one thing, but there's a lot more to hockey than shots on goal."

"And so?" Shola asked. He knew, but he was still hoping.

Greg shook his head. "You're just not ready to play for the Rangers, Shola. Not yet, and maybe not ever."

CHAPTER 7

Off the Sidelines

Shola was crushed. He looked down and shuffled his skates. It seemed like all the other players were looking at him.

Greg smiled. "I have to give you credit, though. I've never seen anyone pick up the game so quickly. Also, I like the way you stuck with the game today. You didn't give up out there. So I'll make you a deal. If you want to keep coming to practices, and you keep getting better . . . well, maybe you can get in a game later in the season. That's not a promise," Greg told him, "just a maybe."

It took a moment for the words to sink in. "You, you'd do that for me?"

Greg laughed. "Of course. But you've got to promise that you'll work hard."

"I promise, coach. I really do."

"Okay, then, get changed. I've got some paperwork that your parents have to sign. Bring it back and I'll see you at next practice."

Paperwork. There was a consent form that his parents would have to sign. But how could Shola tell them?

The answer was very simple: he couldn't. After thinking about it all night, Shola signed the form himself. *What kind of person would do this?* he asked himself. But still he signed his father's name.

Over the next few weeks Shola worked very hard. Every morning he went out to practise his skating. Three times a week he went to practice after school. "To watch Turner," he told his parents. And once a week, after skating and practice he would meet Greg for one-on-one coaching.

One day, after practice, Greg asked Shola to stay behind. Shola skated over to where Greg was standing by the boards.

"Big game this weekend against the Stingers," said Greg. "The playoffs are coming up. They're in first place, you know."

Shola nodded. He had seen the Stingers play and they were a good team.

Greg went on. "Turner's winger sprained his ankle at school. Looks like he won't be able to play. So I guess we're going to need a replacement."

It took a moment to sink in, then Shola looked up at Greg. The coach was smiling. "You mean me, Coach?"

"You're ready, Shola," Greg told him. "You've been working hard and you deserve a chance."

"I'll try hard," Shola said.

"I know you will," Greg replied.

Shola's felt as if his skates didn't touch the ice as he skated off.

That Saturday, Shola was as nervous as he had ever been. Skating around during the warm-up, he was shaking. He kept looking into the crowd, afraid

that his parents might show up. At last the referee blew his whistle to start the game.

Shola's first shift started well. His team moved into the Stingers' end. Then Turner made a good pass to Shola. But before Sola could pass back, two Stingers caught him in the corner. They checked him off the puck. Then a long pass up the wing got to an open Stinger. The player got the puck and skated toward the Rangers' net. All at once the Stingers had two players skating in against one.

Shola and the other Rangers skated hard to get back, but it was too late. With a few passes back and forth, the Stingers scored an easy goal.

After their shift, Greg came over to talk to Shola. "Remember," he said "play defence first. Keep your man covered and wait for your chance."

Shola nodded, trying hard to catch his breath. For the next few shifts he focused on doing just what Greg said.

At the end of the first period, one of the Rangers' other lines scored. That evened the score at 1–1. In the second period, Turner scored a great goal but the Stingers soon struck back. Late in the third period the score was tied at three.

Turner and Shola's line went out, shouting a cheer to each other. Turner won a face-off and went racing away. As he crossed the blue line, Turner sent a pass wide and another Ranger took a hard shot. The Stingers' goalie thrust out his left leg and made a toe save. Then he kicked the puck off to the other wing.

Shola's eyes went wide. The puck was coming at him, and the goalie was well out of position.

Shola picked up the puck, aiming for the wide-open net. The goalie saw the shot coming and began to move. Shola drew back to hit. The goalie dove across the net, reaching out with his blocker. Shola slammed his stick into the puck. Slowly, perfectly, the puck went sailing over the goalie – and into the net.

Shola had scored! It was his first goal ever in a real game.

No one was more surprised than Shola himself. He threw his hands in the air just as Turner grabbed him in a bear hug. The rest of the Rangers all joined in as well, whooping with joy. There was less than a minute left on the clock. Surely this was the winning goal.

Shola waited on the bench as the final seconds ticked by. The Stingers got two more shots but the Rangers' goalie saved them with no problem. When the final buzzer sounded, the whole team cheered.

In the dressing room Greg called for everyone's attention.

"All right boys," he said "great game today. Everyone worked hard and I'm really proud of all

of you. All of you. But I've just got a special thank-you for one guy." He reached down and pulled a box from under a bench.

"We had a new teammate today. Nobody knew how he'd work out. I doubt that he even knew himself. But on his first day, this guy scored the winning goal. How about that?"

There were cheers from all the players.

Greg reached down into the box and took out a package, tossing it over to Shola. "Welcome to the Rangers, Shola."

Shola opened the package and held up what was inside. It was a brand new Rangers jacket, just like the one Turner wore.

"Three cheers for Shola!" he heard Turner yell.

The cheers rang in Shola's ears. But what could he do with the Rangers jacket? If his parents ever saw him wearing it, Shola would be grounded for life.

CHAPTER 8

The Blue Jacket

Shola couldn't wear the jacket home, so he left it with Turner. He made up an excuse, a lie about not accepting gifts in his family. Then he felt bad again. He had lied to his parents, and now he was lying to his best friend.

Still, Shola loved the jacket. He loved being on the team. Walking to school with Turner, he was getting a few surprised looks. Wearing the jacket made him feel even prouder.

"Wow, Shola! Love the jacket," Janna said, as Shola walked up. "I hear you're on the team."

Shola shrugged. "It's nothing."

"Nothing? That's not what I heard," Janna replied. "I heard you scored the winning goal in your first game. That's pretty amazing."

Shola didn't know what to say. He shrugged again, feeling awkward. He was always awkward with girls. "Yeah, well, maybe I got a bit lucky."

Janna laughed. "Or maybe you're just a good player, Shola. Give yourself some credit."

Just then Shola heard a loud voice from across the courtyard. "Ha! Look at that. Looks like the Rangers will give jackets out to anybody these days."

Shola turned to see Keith and his gang. A few of them were wearing the green Chargers jacket.

"What did you do to get that jacket, barefoot boy? Carry some sticks? Fill some water bottles? Bring them some bananas?" His friends all laughed.

Shola stiffened. "Actually," he said, "I made the team."

Keith was shocked. "No way. You? The Rangers must be desperate for players."

Janna stepped forward. "He scored the winning goal against the Stingers."

"Did he now? Well, it was beginner's luck, if you ask me. Did it bounce off your pads or what?"

"Not quite," said Shola "Actually I. . . ."

"Actually," said Keith poking a finger into Shola's chest, "you got lucky. I can't wait for this weekend. I'll show you what real hockey is all about."

Then there was a new voice. "What's that Keith? Cheap shots and poor losers?" Shola saw Turner walking up to them.

Keith stepped back. He game Turner a nasty smile. "Hey, cripple, how's your arm?"

Turner came over to stand beside Shola. "The arm is fine, Keith. I'll show you *how* fine it is on Saturday."

"Maybe you better watch out or you might not make it to Saturday, cripple."

"Oh, I'll make it." Turner smiled. "As long as I don't turn my back on you and your punks."

Keith formed a fist with one hand. "Oh yeah? Maybe I'll have to teach you a lesson right now."

Turner and Shola both dropped their bags and

stood together. Keith's friends closed in around them. The fight was just about to start when they heard a voice shouting at them.

"Okay, cut it out!" A teacher was hurrying across the yard toward them. Keith and his friends took a step back.

"You're both lucky," said Keith under his breath. "You two would have been toast."

"We'll see you on Saturday, jerk," Turner replied.

"I'm looking forward to it, cripple."

Saturday arrived all too soon. Shola and Turner were in the Rangers' dressing room, tying their skates.

"Keep your eyes open," Turner was saying. "That's the thing about Keith. Just keep your eyes open. You can get out of his way if you see him coming."

Shola was a bit unsure. "*If* you see him?"

Turner laughed. "Yeah, he's pretty fast and can skate up on your back. So just stay cool. If you're scared of him and you back off, he'll take advantage of it."

Shola remembered the goal that Keith had scored in road hockey. "Don't worry," he said, "I won't give him any room."

Turner and Shola's line started the game. Keith was on defence for the Chargers. The big guy was doing his best to take runs at both of them.

Back on the bench, Shola looked at Turner. "He's running after us, getting angry. We can use that to our advantage."

Turner smiled. "I know what you mean."

On their next shift, Shola and Turner passed the

puck back and forth. Keith followed them around, trying his best to hit one of them. Keith kept going way out of position, and that gave them an opening. Once, just after Keith went flying past, Shola passed to Turner. In a flash, Turner went in on a breakaway and scored.

After that, the Chargers' coach had a few words with Keith on the bench. Keith had his head down and was nodding. It looked like he was admitting his mistake. From that point on, Keith seemed to forget about chasing after Shola and Turner. Then the big guy scored a goal in the second period to tie the game. Later, the Chargers went ahead. But early in the third period, the Rangers scored twice to make it 3–2.

That's when Shola chased Keith into the Chargers' corner. Skating as fast as he could, Shola lowered his shoulder and hit Keith in the chest. It was a perfect body check that pushed Keith off the puck.

Shola passed to Turner behind the net, then headed for the front. Turner passed back and Shola hit the puck with all his might. He watched as it flew into the net.

"Way to go!" Turner screamed, just as the buzzer went off to end the game.

There was a big cheer from the team, and from the stands, but Shola didn't hear it. He raised his arms in triumph but quickly felt a whack on his upper arm. Then came the jolt of pain.

Shola went down, holding his arm. The referee blew his whistle and cleared the players away. He stood in front of Keith and pointed him off the ice. Then Greg came sliding over from the bench.

"Shola, are you okay?" the coach asked as he reached his side.

"I think so." Shola was still holding his arm, the pain making him wince.

"We'll have to get you back to the dressing room. Can you skate okay?"

"Yeah, I'll make it."

Then Turner skated up beside him. "That must have hurt," his friend said.

"Still hurts," Shola grunted. "But it could have been worse. I could have missed the goal."

Turner helped him up and supported him as

they went slowly off the ice. The crowd gave Shola a big cheer. He was feeling pretty good, despite the pain . . . until he looked up.

Up in the stands were his parents, staring down at him. Suddenly the pain in his arm was nothing compared with the pain in his heart.

Back in the dressing room, Greg could see the damage. A big bruise was already forming. Keith had hit him right in the spot where the elbow pad and the shoulder pad came together.

"Well, I don't think it's broken," Greg was saying. "It would be swelling up more if it was. My hunch is that your arm will be a bit stiff for a few days. And you're sure to have a nasty bruise."

Turner just laughed. "No gain without pain, Shola. And that was a really nice goal." Turner began laughing.

That's when the door to the dressing room flew open.

"I'm glad you find this funny, young man. We do not!"

Shola turned his head. There were his parents, standing in the doorway.

"Mom, I'm okay, really."

"Well, I *am* glad for that, Shola." His mother stomped her foot on the floor. "But you will not be playing this game any more. You understand me? No more hockey."

"And you lied to us," said his father. "You said you were skating, not playing hockey."

Shola looked at them both. "But I can't quit now."

His father shook his head. His mother glared at him. She was as angry as Shola had ever seen her. "You will do as you're told, young man. From now on, you will do as you are told!"

CHAPTER 9

No More Hockey?

Shola stayed silent all the way home. His mother was the one who talked. She raged about this violent game and the boys who played it.

"Hockey is a game for thugs and bullies," she said, "and you are neither of those things. You will not play this game any more. Do you understand me? This is an ugly game, a dangerous game. You will stop!"

"No more lies," added his father. "We did not

bring you to this country to start lying to us. We are your parents. We deserve the truth, if you remember what that is."

Shola knew it was useless to try and explain. Yes, hockey was dangerous. But it was also fast and exciting. Yes, he had lied. But what choice did he have? And now, just when Shola had learned to play – and play well – they were pulling him out.

It wasn't fair. None of it was fair.

So Shola moped. His arm ached. He didn't want to go to school. He sat around the house and watched TV. He said nothing to his parents – no excuses, nothing. Their house was silent.

At last, Shola's father sat down beside him. "Son," he said, "it will do you no good to act like this. Your life isn't over just because you can't play hockey."

"I can't help it," Shola told him. "I loved playing hockey. You can't understand. It means so much to me."

"Really? What does it mean?"

Shola looked up at his father. "When we came here I was so lonely. I never told you, but everything

74

was so different. I felt so out of place. And then I made a friend – *one* friend – and learned how to play this game."

"Against our wishes," said his father.

"Yes, I know. But this is something that I can do, something I am good at. It makes me feel the same as the other kids. It makes it feel right to be here."

Shola's father looked over at his son. He knew exactly what he was saying. He, too, felt lost and lonely in this new land. It was hard for all of them.

"Shola, I know your mother well. She is very

angry right now but she will cool off. Give me a few days and I will have a talk with her. I will do what I can."

It took more than a few days. Shola missed two practices and a Saturday game. It seemed like hockey was over for him. Shola was in despair.

One night, while Shola was studying, his father called to him.

"Shola, come here," said his father. "Your mother and I have talked. We have had a call from your coach and Turner's father. Now your mother wants to talk to you."

Shola went to the living room. The big new TV was on, but no one was watching. Shola's mother was looking at him.

"You're not happy, Shola," she said.

Shola nodded. She knew perfectly well how he felt.

"You don't care about school or homework or anything. You walk around the house like a dead man."

"I just wanted to play hockey," Shola said quietly. "That's all. Just one thing."

"Why is this so important?" she asked. "We didn't bring you to this country to get beaten up on a sheet of ice. It is such a foolish game."

"No, Mother," Shola said with a weary sigh. "It's a game that people play here. It's a way for me to fit in, to belong. Do you understand? It's not just the game, it's more than that."

His father hit the "mute" button and the room went silent. No one spoke. Shola and his father both looked at his mother.

"I don't like this," Shola's mother said at last. "I don't like this game, and I don't like your lying. But I can't stand to see you moping like this. If it takes hockey to make you happy, then go play this game."

"Do you mean it?" Shola asked.

"Just don't get hurt," his mother said. "I mean, don't get hurt *again*."

The playoffs started a few weeks later. The Rangers had won all their games. Now they were up against the Stingers in the semi-finals. The Rangers all trained hard that week. Shola and Turner even put in some extra time in Turner's garage. They practised shots at the painted goalie. They even painted a Stingers' shirt on him.

The air was tense in the dressing room before the game. Turner and Shola dressed without saying much. Dean, who played left wing on their line, came over to talk to them.

"It's time to pull out the special move," Dean said. They had been working on a new play in practice.

"Okay, but we've got to pick our moment," said Turner. "Wait for my signal."

The game started at a fast pace. Both teams went all out to get the first goal. Both goalies made great saves as the shots came at them, hard and fast.

Shola went flat out, skating up and down his wing. He kept chasing the puck, checking and getting checked like a pro.

No one scored in the first period, nor the second. Despite some great shots and plays, the two teams went into third period tied 0–0.

A few minutes into the period, Dean started skating with the puck. Soon he got it out of the

Rangers' end and passed to Turner. Turner circled as the Stingers rushed back to defend. That left the Rangers' end clear. Turner looked at both Shola and Dean. Then he nodded. This was it. He gave the signal for their play.

Shola and Dean took off across the ice toward each other. They crossed in the centre and Turner passed to Dean. He skated toward the boards, then cut back inside. Meanwhile Shola did the same thing on the other side of the ice – but without the puck. As Dean and Shola rushed toward each other again, their eyes met. Shola nodded. Dean lifted his stick. Shola took the puck.

The two Stingers who were marking them skated right into each other. The pair crashed backwards onto the ice. That gave Shola a second or two. He turned and passed the puck to Turner. Turner went shooting through the gap created by the fallen Stingers. He went in on goal, then faked twice to the right. The fake sent the goalie the wrong way. Then Turner slid to his left and put the puck in the net.

The whole Rangers team yelled and the crowd

cheered loudly. Shola, Turner and Dean came together, giving high fives all around.

The game was over, really, but the Rangers scored one more goal before the buzzer. The Rangers won, 2–0.

Shola and Turner grabbed each other. They screamed as the whole team skated from the bench to jump on them. The Rangers had won the game and were going to the final. They'd be up against the team that had won in the morning round – the Chargers.

One more time, Shola and Turner would be facing Keith on the ice.

CHAPTER 10

Tie Score

Shola could hardly think about school that week. At lunch, he and Turner could talk about nothing but the game to come. Even Janna was excited.

"I'm coming to the game with Alex," she told them. "I can't wait to see you guys crush those goons."

Later, Keith came walking by.

"Hey, cripple," he said. "I've got a great spot picked out at home for the trophy."

Turner snapped back, "They don't give a trophy for second place."

"Very funny, cripple. But we'll see who's laughing on Saturday. Remember, it's hard to laugh when you're in pain."

On Saturday, Shola woke up early. He was jumpy and restless all day. Even in the car he couldn't sit still. His father had to tell him twice to stop playing with the radio and sit back in his seat. His mother just shook her head.

"I can't believe I'm coming to watch my son play hockey," she said, shaking her head. "Shola, promise me you won't get hurt. Just promise me."

"I won't get hurt," Shola said out loud. But in a whisper he added two words: "I hope."

As the Rangers were getting dressed, Greg went around the room to talk to each player. Soon he sat on the bench beside Turner and Shola. "Hey guys, how are you doing?" he said.

Shola and Turner both nodded. "We're ready," said Turner.

"Good. Now listen. You two have been scoring well, but I want to try and get a little more scoring from our other lines. So I'm going to try something. Turner, I want you to centre Pete and Rico. Caleb is going to move up and play centre with Dean and Shola."

"You sure that's a good idea?" Turner asked.

"My call," Greg replied. "Unless you want to take over my job."

Greg gave a little speech but Shola barely heard a word of it. He wondered how he could possibly play without Turner.

Turner broke into his thoughts. "Don't worry," he said, clapping Shola on the shoulder. "It's all the same game. You'll be fine."

Shola took a deep breath and nodded. "Oh, I'll be okay," he said. "I was just worried about you. Who's going to watch your back?"

They both laughed and headed out on the ice. The cold air seemed to clear Shola's head. Suddenly he wasn't nervous, just full of energy. The two teams warmed up in their own ends. One end was a swirl of blue Rangers, the other of green Chargers. When the referee blew his whistle for the game to start, Shola made his way to the bench.

Soon he could see the Chargers' game plan. They were out to hit the Rangers' players as often and as hard as they could. Shola's teammates were getting knocked over whenever they touched the puck – and sometimes when they didn't. Keith ran into Turner at one point, knocking him into the boards. Turner bounced right back up again, but he was hurt. Shola could tell.

At last, one of the Chargers got a penalty. Shola's line went out for the power play.

Shola found it tough to play with the new guys. Turner would always push forward and Shola always knew where he would be. The new centre would hang back and play a more defensive style. So Shola's passes went wild. The few shots he got went wide of the net. The first period ended 0–0. The Rangers couldn't score.

Early in the second period, Keith knocked a Rangers' player off the puck. Keith grabbed the puck and dashed in on goal. Then he cut in front of the defence and fired a low shot past the Rangers' goalie. 1–0.

Shola watched the Chargers cheer. He wanted to

do something, but he was stuck on the bench.

On his next shift, Shola saw Keith in the corner. The big guy was waiting for the puck with his head down. Shola darted toward him, his body tense. Keith took a pass, turned, and fired the puck.

Shola could have stopped himself if he really wanted to, but at that moment he didn't care. He pushed hard with his shoulder into Keith's chest.

Keith grunted. He looked at Shola. He felt the pain. Then Keith's feet left the ice. He sailed backwards, into the boards.

The referee blew his whistle and Shola was sent off for his first-ever penalty. Two months ago, and Shola would have felt ashamed. Now he felt anger. *Keith deserved it*, he said to himself.

The Chargers used the power play and swarmed around the Rangers net. Shola watched from the penalty box as they took shot after shot. Finally, the Rangers' goalie was out of position. The puck was slapped past him into the net. It was now 2–0.

Shola had his head down as the team skated back to the bench. That goal was all his fault. He should have stopped himself from hitting Keith. He should have been smarter. But he had been selfish and had let the team down.

Shola sadly took his place on the bench beside Turner. His friend didn't even look up. Greg made his way over to them and Shola feared the worst.

"Hey, guys," said Greg. "I don't think my new plan is working. If I put you guys back together, can you promise me some things?"

Shola and Turner looked at each other.

"Okay, you're both on at the start of the third. Shola, you stay cool. We need you on the ice, not in the box."

"No problem, coach," said Shola. With just a few words, his spirits had lifted. His whole outlook on the game had changed. Their team had a whole period to go and were only two goals down. Shola knew that as long as he was playing with Turner, they could do it.

They skated out together to start the third period. Keith was on the ice for the Chargers. He gave Shola a look before the face-off. "I'm coming after you, boy," the look said.

The puck dropped. Right away, Turner and

Shola took it down into the Chargers' end. Shola got it in the corner and looked up in time to see Keith charging toward him. He stepped to one side and let him go by. Then he looked up and saw Turner in front of the net. Shola passed and Turner slapped the puck past the Chargers' goalie into the net.

The Rangers' fans cheered. Turner and Shola had been back together for less than a minute and had already scored a goal.

A bit later, Shola raced out of his own end with the puck. Keith was skating back and closing in fast. As Shola approached, Keith brought his stick up. He was holding it between his hands, ready to hit Shola as hard as he could.

At the last second Shola ducked. He made contact with Keith's knees and that knocked both of them over.

Keith hit the boards with a crunching sound. But Shola had no time to look at him. Shola saw that there was a clear path to the Chargers net. He glanced at the referee. Yes, he had tripped Keith, but it had been in self-defence. If Keith had hit him with the illegal cross-check, it would have sent him flying.

The referee's arm stayed down – no penalty.

Shola took off, skating in on goal. He moved to the right, drawing the goalie to that side. Then he fired a pass over to Turner who was wide open in front. Turner scored with a shot to the top corner. It was 2–2.

From that point on, the game got very tense. Both teams played big defence, doing their best not to make any mistakes. The clock ticked down as they struggled. It looked like they would be heading for overtime.

With about thirty seconds left, the Chargers won a face-off deep in the Rangers' end. Greg sent Turner and Shola over the boards. "Listen up, guys," he said. "Keep it simple, okay? Don't take any chances."

Shola looked up as he waited for the face-off. Keith was waiting on the blue line. He was the man Shola had to cover. The puck was dropped and the Chargers' centre sent it back toward Keith. Shola took off toward him. Keith took his stick back and put everything he had behind the shot.

Shola blocked the shot with his shin pads. He took off after the puck, catching up to it at centre ice. He had a breakaway. A few more strides and he was closing in on goal.

The goalie looked very much alone, way out in front of his net.

If only my old friends could see me now, Shola said to himself. He was skating on a sheet of ice. He was playing a game none of his friends had ever heard of. He was playing this game in a cold, cold country, so far from where he was born.

And now, he might just score the winning goal.

Shola glanced up at the clock. Twenty seconds. Plenty of time. He thought for a second, then launched his attack. Shola cut to his right and then to his left. This brought him across the face of the goal and forced the goalkeeper to move with him. This had been his favourite move in soccer, back in his old country. Why wouldn't it work in hockey?

Shola cut in front. The puck seemed to slide off his stick and back into his skates.

The goalie froze. His eyes lit up as he saw Shola's "mistake." He got ready to launch himself at the

puck, to clear it out of the way. But just as the goalie threw himself forward, Shola used his back skate to kick the puck up to his stick.

There was the net, wide and empty.

Shola smiled. The goalie gritted his teeth.

Shola paused for a second, then fired the puck into the middle of the net.

There was screaming from the stands and cheers from his teammates. Shola raised his arms in triumph and skated back toward his team. Turner reached him first and bowled him over. The rest of the team piled on top. Shola could barely breathe on the bottom of the pile, but it was all wonderful. He had scored the winning goal. He had come halfway around the world for this moment.

Twenty seconds later the game was over. The Rangers were the champions and Shola was their hero. The whole team gathered around and patted him on the back. Then they went to shake hands with the Chargers.

As he went through the line, Shola saw Keith approaching. They stopped in front of each other. Keith looked angry at losing the game. Shola tensed, fearing the worst.

"Good game, Shola," was all Keith said. He put his hand out for Shola to shake.

Shola shook his hand, slightly stunned. "You too," he said. "See you next year."

Shola saw the nasty grin return to Keith's face. "Count on it," he said, moving down the line.

The team went to get their trophies, with great cheers from the stands. When they skated off to the dressing room, Shola saw his parents. They were in the stands, just above the glass shield. His dad had a camera and was busy taking pictures. His mom, to Shola's surprise, was smiling.

"You were wonderful!" she screamed.

"You scored the winning goal!" shouted his father. "You go change and we'll celebrate."

Now Shola was embarrassed. Why did parents have to act like that?

"I can't," Shola yelled back. "The team is going out for pizza."

Shola's parents looked at each other. His mother seemed a bit hurt, but his father just put his arm around her.

"You go ahead," said his father. "It's important. It's more important than winning, you know."

Shola did know. As he headed to the dressing room, Turner came up and slapped him on the shoulder. "Your parents still mad?" Turner asked.

"Not any more," Shola told him.

"They're all the same," he said. "All over the world."

If you enjoyed *Shola's Game*, look for these other HIP novels:

Against All Odds
Avalanche
Caught in the Blizzard
Hacker!
Scarface
Street Scene
Tag Team

For more information on the books in the HIP Sr. series contact:

 High Interest Publishing – Publishers of H·I·P Books
407 Wellesley Street East • Toronto, Ontario M4X 1H5
www.hip-books.com